stalked by the irishman

EMMA BRAY

one

Derrick

I GLARE AT THOMAS. We may have been best friends as close as brothers since we were wee lads, but if he touches my Rachel again, he'll lose that hand. The amused twinkle in the asshole's eyes lets me know he notes my irritation. The only reason I've managed to keep myself from jumping out of this chair and barreling over there to rip his hand off hers is that I know Thomas isn't interested in Rachel. It's her friend, Ella, he wants.

And lucky for him my Rachel doesn't look interested in him either. It'd be a real shame to have to murder my best friend.

But I would.

I'd do it in a heartbeat for Rachel.

I'd do anything for her.

My obsession with her borders on madness. I'm totally aware of this, yet I can't do anything to stop it.

I don't want to do anything to stop it.

My life has new meaning and purpose now. Everything that came before seems so empty. I was just going through the motions. Making money, being successful.

But all the money and success in the world doesn't mean anything if I don't have my reason for living.

And Rachel is my reason for living.

Only she doesn't know it.

She doesn't know me.

Yes, we've technically met. Once. The day I looked into her caramel-colored eyes and my world tilted on its axis.

The day my obsession wrapped itself around me like a cobra and began to squeeze so tightly I couldn't breathe without feeding it.

The day a stalker was born.

Never in a million years would I have believed I'd

become one of those sick creeps who watches a woman obsessively, yet here I am.

But I'm not a sick creep. That's what I tell myself anyway. I don't just lust after Rachel like some kind of horndog.

No, I *love* her. I love everything about her. The way her hair rivals the rich mocha color of the coffees she brews. The way it sways against her back as she moves. The way she fills out that little black skirt that's a tad too short for my liking in light of all the other men who come in here and get to see her in it daily.

The way her white button-up blouse stretches over her breasts, threatening to pop open at any minute. My Rachel is a tiny little thing, but she's got just enough curves in all the right places to make a man want to throw away his livelihood for just one smile, one toss of her head.

She took my order and made me a coffee. Right here in this very coffee shop that I spend most of my day in now just because she does—much to the annoyance of Thomas.

He's not only my best friend, but he's my business partner as well. Granted, he owns a slightly larger share in the business, but none of that matters to me. I'm not greedy. I'm just thankful he was willing to go into business with me and that we've been able to achieve what we have over here in the States.

I've really been slacking on him ever since I saw Rachel, though. I know I'm leaving the burden of the operations on him, but I can't help it.

I can't seem to tear myself away from this coffee shop. Away from *her*.

I sit here all day at this tiny-ass little table that's too dainty for a man of my stature on the best of days and try to work on my laptop just so I can steal surreptitious glances over at my tiny angel every now and then.

This place is always jumping with business, so it's easy for me to get lost in the sea of faces, especially since I always make sure to sit over here in the back corner that's half hidden in the shadows.

I'm sure she doesn't remember me. Too many faces come in and out of here. It's every professional's spot to drop in for coffee throughout the day since it's so conveniently located to all our high-rises down here.

I've only allowed myself to be served by her just that one time. Since then, I've kept my distance, only approaching the counter to place an order when she's on break or otherwise engaged.

It's insane, I know. My whole body literally aches

for her, yet I deny myself the simple pleasure of the smallest interaction with her.

I must be a masochist because I put myself through torture every day watching her, listening to her sweet voice as she talks to *other* people, smiles at *other* people.

For God's sake, how long are you going to keep stalking her? Why don't you just go over there and ask her out?

Thomas' voice keeps echoing throughout my head.

Why don't I? That's the crux of the issue, isn't it? I don't rightly know.

It's not that I'm intimidated like some high school lad. Granted, I'm certainly not the cocky bastard that Thomas is, but I'm not lacking in confidence or anything.

No, contrary to what Thomas thinks, I'm just biding my time.

I think it's more that I'm a planner, an observer if you will. I like to gather all the facts and know every-thing before I make my move. I know from experience if I go rushing into things ruled by my emotions, it'll get me in trouble every time. I was known for being a bit of a hothead back in our mother country. But here,

I got a fresh start to calm down and do things sensibly.

But everything about Rachel makes me want to lose my senses and act on pure, primal instinct. I think the real reason I hold myself back from her is because I *know* one touch is all it's going to take to unleash my inner animal. My obsession for her will only amplify once I touch her, and then I might scare her off.

And I don't know how I'll be able to live in a world without her. I sure as hell won't be able to watch her be with another man. I'll selfishly run all men who dare approach her away and keep her single forever if she doesn't want me.

And see? That's completely fucked up. It's thinking like *that*...that's why I'm keeping my distance from her.

My eyes find her across the coffee shop. I caress her with my eyes like I long to do with my fingertips. My hands tighten around the edge of the table as I drink her up. I don't come here for the coffee. No, I come here for my daily shot of her. I can live without caffeine. That's not what I need to survive.

I need *her*. I need her so badly I don't know how much longer I'm going to be able to hold back.

And frankly, that scares me a bit. I'm terrified —*terrified*—of scaring her away. I think I'll die if go overboard with her and freak her out so she thinks I'm a psycho and doesn't want anything to do with me.

That's why I'm keeping my distance and staying off her radar.

At least for now.

* * *

She lives on Highland Avenue. She doesn't know it, but I walk her home every day.

I make sure to stay plenty of steps behind her. Can't chance her seeing me, but I have to make sure she's safe.

I frown as I once again take in the decrepit-looking building she lives in. It goes against everything in me to know that my tiny angel is living in a subpar place like this. She deserves the best of the best. I want to put her in a penthouse overlooking all of the city. I want to spoil her with diamonds and designer clothing, though I already know just from observing her these past few weeks that's not the kind of stuff she's into. No, my girl is practical. She was never handed a silver spoon, and she works hard for everything she has.

While her best friend, the girl that Thomas suddenly seems to be so taken with, was lucky enough to come into an inheritance that she used to start her yoga studio with, fate didn't show my girl such a kind hand. She's been on her own ever since she turned eighteen and migrated out of the foster care system. I still don't know what all of her hopes and dreams are since I can't get close enough to ask her, but I know that she's a hard worker.

She's twenty-one, and she's one of the few who was able to land a full-time job at the coffee shop where she works all day. I don't know if that's what she plans on doing for the rest of her life or if it's just what she has to do to make ends meet.

If I had my way, she wouldn't ever have to lift a finger for the rest of her life. She wouldn't have to scrape by, running herself ragged and standing on her feet all day just to make ends meet. I'd take care of her if she just let me.

I know it's the cliche kind of crap heard in cheesy love songs, but I'd give her the world if she was just mine. Hell, even if she's not mine, I want to give her everything her little heart desires. I want to make her happy—even if she's not with me.

My heart twists within me at the thought of her happiness hinging on another man, though. The only condition I have is that I cannot—I simply *cannot*—see her with another man. It would destroy me.

You might as well put a bullet through my head right now.

I watch as her neighbor comes out of his door right when Rachel reaches hers. My hands ball into fists. Typical. If there's one thing about this asshole, it's that he's thoroughly predictable.

I know what the fucker wants, and what he wants is *mine*.

My entire body vibrates with the need to bash his face in. Swell his eyes up so shut he can't look at her.

I'm already pissed the fuck off that this asshole lives right next door to her. But what makes it even worse is how the fucker always tries to get a word in with her any chance he can. I swear I think he times whenever she gets off work so he can oh so casually make an appearance and try to speak with her.

He's skating on thin ice. I've had about as much as I can take out of him. The only thing that's saving him is Rachel and her disinterest in him.

I can see the tiredness in my Rachel's eyes all the way from where I'm standing in the shadows. But this idiot can't take a hint, and she's too kind to just tell him to fuck off.

Fortunately for her, I'm not. I don't have a problem telling every motherfucker who looks at her the wrong way to get lost, and I mentally pencil in a visit with this asshat. He has yet to have the pleasure of a meeting with me, but he's just earned himself one. Hell, I've let his advances toward my girl slide too many times as it is.

I tilt my head in their direction to better hear what he's saying to her. I clench my fists, rage pumping through me when I hear him asking her if she'd like to come over and have dinner with him some night, that she must be so exhausted when she gets off work and he always makes too much—like he's just being a friendly neighbor, kind and considerate, when he and I both know better. I can read the intent in his eyes clear as day.

I stand with bated breath waiting for her answer.

I let out an exhale of relief whenever she promptly shoots him down, thanking him but saying no.

Good girl, Rachel. You may have just saved a man's life tonight.

There's no way in hell I'm going to let her be in an apartment with another man, especially one who I know is trying to get inside her pants.

The imbecile's shoulders slump, and he slinks his way back into his apartment with a sad glance back over his shoulder.

Yeah, that's right asshole. Keep it moving. She doesn't want anything to do with you. Look at the bright side, though. It's your lucky night. I don't have to break both your legs. We'll still be having that little chat tomorrow, though.

I walk around to the side of the apartment where I can see her window, staying out of sight in the darkened alley that gives me a clear view up to her.

I usually get one last glimpse of her moving around her apartment before she closes the blinds. I wait for her to come into view now. I need that last glimpse of her to tide me over to tomorrow morning.

My heart leaps into my chest when she comes into view. I'm like an overeager dog jumping at the sight of its owner. I wait to get that one last look at her pretty face, but tonight for some reason—maybe it's because she's too tired or too distracted—she doesn't close the blinds.

My pulse is thundering in my throat as I watch her walk through her apartment, slipping off her shirt and her pants as she goes, flinging them onto the floor.

My mouth goes dry at the sight of her. She's wearing a simple white bra and white cotton panties, but damn if this sight of her in the those simple little underthings isn't more pornographic than the fanciest bustier set.

I clench my teeth together so tightly I'm surprised I don't shatter my molars. I'm both aroused and royally pissed off. Why the fuck is she getting undressed with her window blinds still open? Any pervert could walk by and see her like this.

My eyes can't stop rolling over her creamy skin and the way her tiny waist dips in and then flares out over her gently sculpted hips. I trail my gaze down over her shapely legs and calves, all the way down to her dainty little feet. I can see the bright pink nail polish on her toes all the way out here.

My eyes rove back up to the curve of those generous breasts that almost look too big for her tiny frame. That beautiful chocolate, mocha-colored hair falls in front of her shoulders as she bends over to pick her clothes up off the floor.

I bite back a groan at the tease, knowing that her breasts are about to spill out of those cups, yet my view is obscured by that silky hair hanging down over them. It's curling and wrapping around them as if to taunt me.

She turns away from me and unsnaps her bra, revealing her beautiful bare back.

I don't see the front of her breasts, but I can just imagine them bobbing free, and I lengthen painfully in my pants, my fully erect cock now pressing up against my zipper.

My breathing turns ragged, and I stand there with

a raging hard on, aching and dying for some sort of relief but unwilling to leave until I see that she's turned that damned light off so that everyone can't see inside her apartment.

I bite back a groan when she puts on a tiny tank top that reveals a patch of skin between her panties and bellybutton. I admire the slight jiggle of her ass as she walks over to her fridge and grabs some sort of pre-made meal. She pops it in the microwave and then pulls it out, only taking a couple of bites before she pushes the rest away, leaving it sitting on the counter.

I frown. She works too hard and doesn't eat enough.

Fortunately, Rachel is an early to bed, early to rise kind of girl. It doesn't take her long to slide into bed and kill the lights.

Only when there's nothing but darkness coming from her window do I walk back over to where my car's parked discreetly a couple of blocks down from her apartment. Probably not wise to leave my luxury vehicle untended in this type of neighborhood for long, but keeping an eye on my girl is more important than any car.

I'd wreck one every day if she asked me to.

As usual, though, I'm not gone long enough for anyone to mess with my vehicle.

I'm still swollen, my balls heavy with my seed when I get back inside the privacy of my vehicle.

Fuck, I can't wait.

I release my aching cock and begin jerking off to the mental images of Rachel that are now burned into my brain.

I imagine how pink and rosy her nipples must be, how hard they would be if I were to lick them, the little whimpers and sounds of pleasure she would make with me sucking them. I remember the way her sweet little mound looked in those innocent white panties. I wonder if they were wet, what she tastes like.

Christ Almighty, just the thought of that is enough to hurl me over the edge. I come with a strangled moan, my head falling back against the seat as I bust harder than I think I've ever busted before in my life.

After I'm cleaned up, I sit there staring up at her dark window for a few more moments.

My jaw ticks with irritation. She has no idea that a man is sitting down here in his car jacking off to thoughts of her after being treated with her innocent peep show.

The thought that someone else could have seen

her undress makes my jaw harden. I squint and survey up and down the street, relaxing only a bit when I don't see anyone else in sight—and I'm specifically checking for people hidden in the shadows like me.

Satisfied that no one else witnessed my girl's nearly naked body, I start up my car.

One thing is for sure.

This is never going to happen again.

I'll be taking care of those blinds tomorrow.

And I still haven't forgotten my meeting with her too-friendly neighbor. That shit's going to stop too.

two

Rachel

I'M BEAT. After standing on my feet all day and running back and forth to try to fulfill customers' orders as quickly as I can, I'm just exhausted. Who would have thought that making coffee all day would be such a physically demanding job? It's just go, go, go from the time I walk in the door.

The coffee shop is in a prime location. Business is always hopping.

But I honestly love that about it. I like to be so busy that my work passes by in a quick blur. My day goes quickly. I would hate it if I did something super boring and my day drug by. Plus, this might sound totally lame, but I honestly love being a barista.

I've always had a passion for coffee. Call me a basic bitch, but I'm the girl who shares memes of coffee on her social media profiles.

I love coffees with sweet creams, hot or cold. I love the coffee shop vibe. I just love everything about it.

I'm honestly a little bit jealous of my friend Rachel. She lucked into getting enough money in an inheritance so that she could afford to follow her dreams and start her own yoga studio.

If only I had had some rich uncle or other relative who left me a nice lump sum of cash where I could have started my very own coffee shop.

Don't get me wrong. I'm very grateful to have the job that I do. Most of my co-workers don't get to work full time, but I somehow finagled my way into it.

My job pays the bills. And it's not like it's all about the money for me or anything, but I would really like to own my own place and do things my way. I'd like to be able to experiment and come up with new drinks.

I can already envision everything in my mind. The cute displays I would have. Everything I would do to make my coffee shop experience better than all the rest.

Maybe offer some live music. Maybe have some

guest speakers, some of the city's trendiest poets and authors, do some readings.

It would be more than just coffee. It would be the experience. Unfortunately, I don't have the capital to start my own shop, though. And with the way my saving is going, I won't have enough to do that anytime soon. I'll be an old lady before I can ever even make a down payment on owning my own shop.

Oh well. The pay might not be amazing, but at least I'm doing something I love doing.

My shoulders sag with relief when I finally remove my name tag and clock out.

I'm going to have to do something about this exhaustion, though. I'm running myself ragged. Whenever a co-worker needs some time off or can't come in for whatever reason, I always jump to cover their shift, which means I end up doing more than my full-time hours, which is great because I love the overtime pay, but at the same time, I know that something has to give. That fact is made even more prominent to me when I leave my shift and find myself fighting back a yawn. I lift my hand up and try to stifle it.

Nope, doesn't work. This yawn is coming whether I want it to or not.

I keep my mouth covered, my eyes closing instinctively as I yawn.

That split second of having my eyes shut while I'm still walking is just enough for me to lose my balance. My heart leaps up into my chest when I feel my feet stumble. It certainly doesn't help that the sidewalk is teeming with people rushing home after work so that I'm jostled back and forth.

I flail, trying to regain my balance, but I lose my footing and start falling into traffic.

I look up and panic when I see a car coming straight at me. I close my eyes again—this time on purpose. I hear the blaring of a car horn.

Oh God, this is it. This is how I'm going to die.

You know how people say when you're going to die, your life passes before your eyes?

Nope, nothing like that happens to me.

Instead, all my mind can think about is how ridiculous my death will sound.

What will they write about me in the papers? *Clumsy, overworked woman falls headfirst into traffic.*

I try to brace myself for the impact I know is coming even as my arms are still flailing on instinct as I try in vain to set myself aright and keep myself out of the road.

The impact never comes, though. Instead, everything seems to just stop. I'm just hanging there suspended above the road.

What the hell?

It takes me a minute to register that a pair of big, strong arms are wrapped around me, suspending me in midair, until suddenly I'm yanked backward back onto the sidewalk.

I let out an *oof* as I smash back against something hard as granite.

"Easy there, lass," a deep voice rumbles right in my ear. I feel the reverberations of that voice go clean through my chest where my back is pressed against his body. The sensation is like nothing I've ever experienced. It tingles throughout me like a tiny shock to my system.

When I finally get my footing back under me, his arms gradually release me, and I turn to face him. Big hands come out to steady me with a hand on both of my upper arms. The feeling of those hands on my skin sends tingles shooting down to my fingertips.

I'm shaken from my near-brush with death and am obviously having exaggerated reactions to everything.

I look up to see who my rescuer is. At first, I'm staring at nothing but a massive, broad chest in a white button-up shirt. The top two buttons are left undone, revealing a tan expanse of pure muscle.

A suit jacket covers his arms, but something tells

me those arms are just as hard and muscular as the chest I'm currently staring at. A fresh, woodsy scent wraps itself around me intoxicatingly, and I drag my eyes up that chest over a thick neck and up to a stylishly bearded jaw, a nose that actually looks like it's been broken once before, and then up to the most vibrant pair of green eyes I've ever seen in my entire life.

My breath catches in my throat at their intensity, and I blink. They're a startling shade, like emeralds glimmering down at me. I blink again, my brow furrowing as recognition teases at the back of my brain.

Something about them is so familiar. I've seen these eyes before. I know I have—only I just can't place where.

My face flushes when I finally realize that I've been staring at him, all slack-jawed and starry-eyed probably.

My flush only deepens when I realize that his arms are still gripping onto my shoulders lightly as if he's afraid my clumsy ass is going to fall back into traffic if he releases me.

Hell, I probably would. I feel as if a light wind would be enough to topple me over at this point.

Somehow I manage to speak. "Thanks for saving

me," I let out a nervous laugh. "That could have ended really badly for me if you hadn't been here. I don't know what's wrong with me. Just clumsy, I guess."

He doesn't say anything. He's just staring down at me so freaking intently. My breath catches in my throat again. I can't pinpoint exactly how he's looking at me. All I know is it's a bit unsettling yet thrilling at the same time.

The look in his eyes holds me captive so that all I can do is stare back at him, mesmerized by those green eyes.

I clear my throat and find my voice again, "Do I know you from somewhere?" I ask the question slowly, wracking my brain for where I've seen him before, convinced that I do indeed know him from somewhere.

He blinks then as if pulled from some sort of haze. A look of surprise crosses his face before he finally nods his head slowly, saying gruffly, "Maybe from that coffee shop. I go there sometimes to order a cup. You took my order one day."

Good lord, his voice is all deep and growly and gravelly, and why does it make my toes curl in my sensible black sneakers?

I take in his business attire and nod. Yeah, it makes sense that I probably saw him at the coffee shop. Tons of businesspeople come in to get coffee, and this man is obviously in business. A very profitable one at that if the expensive suit he's wearing is any indication.

Yes, the coffee shop is probably where I've seen him before, but sweet baby Jesus, how could I have ever forgotten this man? The sheer size of him alone is unforgettable. He's got to be at least six foot four, and I'm five foot nothing.

The man is like a giant standing next to me. I have to crane my head back to look up at him.

His hands are like huge paws. One hand could probably span my entire back.

Why does that make my heart race?

I hear myself speaking before I can even register what I'm going to say, "Do you want a cup of coffee?" I ask him, immediately flushing when I realize it sounds like I'm asking him out on a date.

He blinks again, obviously surprised.

"To say thank you, I mean," I elaborate, "you know, for saving my life just now. I'm off work right now, but my apartment is just a few blocks up. I can whip you up a cup there." I trail off when I realize that I'm rambling.

My cheeks flame even hotter than before. Oh my god, he probably thinks I'm some pathetic little fool. This man is gorgeous as hell. He probably has model-type women hanging on his arms every night, and here I am—a stupid little barista—inviting him to my place for a cup of coffee.

What the hell is wrong with me?

I'm mortified, about to die with embarrassment when he finally nods slowly, his eyes never straying from mine as if he's memorizing every detail of my face.

Something about that makes me warm all over.

"Sure," he answers at last. "A cup of coffee sounds good." He pauses before adding, "I'm Derrick, by the way."

I flush again when I realize I invited him to my place without even knowing his name. "Rachel," I manage to say, my voice coming out breathy.

"Rachel," his deep voice rumbles my name, and I detect a slight brogue to the way he rolls the syllables.

I realize I'm staring at him again when he places his hand on the small of my back and moves me so that he's the one standing on the side of the sidewalk closer to traffic. I'm now standing further from the street with his body acting as a barrier between me and the road, almost like he's protecting me from the threat of danger there.

My heart does a little flip within me.

He motions forward with his other hand. "Lead the way, lass," that deep voice rumbles again.

He's Irish. I can tell it in his accent. And now that I look at him more closely, I can see flecks of auburn in his beard.

I peek another glance up at him, noting his size all over again.

This probably isn't the smartest thing I've ever done. Who invites a guy they don't even know over for coffee right off the street?

But surely if he was going to hurt me, he wouldn't have saved me.

Those green eyes see me peeking up at him and capture me again, blazing down at me like green flames.

I feel my face heating again.

I don't know what it is about this man, but he has me all tied into knots.

And now I'm going to be alone with him in my apartment.

Good lord, what have I gotten myself into?

three

Derrick

MY RACHEL HAS GONE silent on me. Whereas she was chattering away in a breathy, almost embarrassed fashion, now she's pensive as she "leads" us to her apartment. Little does she know I could find my way to her apartment and around the inside of it blindfolded. I was just inside it this morning, actually.

I try my best to keep my gaze straight ahead to avoid making her more nervous than she already is, but I'm watching her out of the corner of my eye—a skill that I've honed to perfection over my time observing her in the coffee shop.

I notice the way a strand of her hair falls over the front of her shoulder. And how the end of that hair curls around the bottom of her plump breast. I see the way she keeps nibbling on her lips and taking little peeking glances over at me. She's starting to second-guess her impulsiveness of asking a man she barely knows over to her apartment.

That's good. I was halfway pissed off when she did it myself. I could have been any psycho. It's not smart for her to be inviting strangers over to her house—even if they did just save her life.

Of course, I'm not really a stranger to her, and I'd never harm a hair on her perfect little head. And I'm glad that I'm actually going to be getting closer to my Rachel now. Although this certainly isn't how I planned on inserting myself into her life. Of course, at the rate I was going, who knows when I would have ever decided when the right time was.

My hand was forced when I saw her falling into traffic. I acted on instinct. I saw my whole world crashing down in front of me—literally. And I didn't think. I moved before I could even process it.

My god, my fears about revealing myself to her were right. One touch is all it took. She felt so right in my arms, her perfect little body held up against me. I'm vibrating right now and clenching my fists together to try to hold back the need to touch her again.

Her skin is as soft as rose petals, just like I knew it would be. She smells like warm vanilla beans, all sugary and delicious. Everything about her is so damn sweet and tempting.

I don't try to break the silence. It's all I can do to keep from grabbing her and slinging her over my shoulder to physically cart her back to my place with me where I'll declare my undying love and devotion to her before claiming her like the caveman I suddenly feel like.

We're milling through all the bodies around us on the sidewalk, so it's not really the most conducive environment for carrying on a conversation anyway. And it's a good thing, I suppose, because my throat is closing up on me. I don't even know where to begin, and I'm scared if I open my mouth, everything I feel for this girl is going to come tumbling out.

And then she'll run. She'll think I'm certifiably insane.

Hell, maybe I am. I'm certainly not in my right mind when it comes to her.

"Here we are," she says when we reach her apartment. Her hands are trembling as she puts the key in the doorknob, and I feel my own heartbeat hammering against my ribcage. I'd love to have her trembling with desire beneath me. I'd kiss every inch of her perfect skin and soothe every fear. She'd never have to doubt that she's the most perfect angel to ever grace this earth if she just let me worship her.

"It's not much, but it's home," she explains with an embarrassed wave of her hand once we cross the threshold. I don't even glance around her apartment. I already know what it looks like.

However, I do make sure to put her mind at ease about her humble abode. Don't let the business suit or today's success fool you. I'm definitely no snob. I grew up in more meager circumstances than this, and Rachel's place—though not worthy of her—is pretty substantial considering she's living in this expensive city all on her own and paying all her bills herself with no roommate to help her.

"It's beautiful, lass," I tell her, though in all truth, I'm not really talking about the apartment, nor am I looking at it.

My gaze is honed in on my tiny little angel. She's looking too pretty for words.

She notices my gaze on her, and maybe she picks up on the fact that my compliment wasn't really about the apartment because her cheeks heat with that pretty blush again.

God, I love seeing her cheeks stained pink. I wonder if her entire body will flush like that whenever I have my tongue deep inside her. I feel myself harden and fight to bite back the groan the thought of having my face in between her sweet thighs conjures up.

She moves to turn on a lamp, mumbling an apology for how dark it is in her place and about how something must have happened to her blinds. She couldn't get them to open this morning.

I have to fight back a smirk. I know exactly what happened to those motherfuckers. I fixed them so that I don't have to worry about my girl being too tired or forgetful to close the damn blinds at night. I'm not taking the chance of anyone else getting the kind of show I got last night.

I also noticed her asshole neighbor didn't dare poke his head out of his door tonight. That may have had something to do with my presence next to her, but I think it's more than that. I think he was very receptive to our "business meeting" earlier wherein I informed him not so nicely to back the fuck off, that Rachel was taken, and I better not so much as see him glance in her direction anymore. That as far as he's concerned, she's dead to him.

He was unsurprisingly very receptive to my proposal. Of course, holding a man by the collar of his shirt and snarling the directive in his face tends to have that effect.

It's a very effective mode of doing business, I must say.

I follow her into the kitchen, watching her hips sway as she sets about grinding up some coffee beans.

I already knew this about her. My girl doesn't drink any of that pre-ground shit. And don't even get her started on instant coffee. Stuff that she firmly believes should be illegal to even be called coffee.

"How do you like your coffee?" she gives me a nervous smile from where she's making the brew.

"Cream? Sugar?" she prompts.

I lick my lips and fight back another groan at those words coming from her lips. "Aye, I want lots of cream and sugar, lass." My voice comes out gruff, and her cheeks heat again as she apparently picks up on the double meaning behind my words.

Damn it. If I keep going at this rate and don't reign in my thoughts and put a filter on my mouth, I'm going to have my cock deep inside her snatch before the night is over. And while I'd certainly love nothing more than that, by the way Rachel's hands are trembling, she's probably not ready for anything of that magnitude. I don't know if it's just me that's making her nervous or if she's truly as inexperienced as she seems, but the thought that my Rachel might actually be a virgin has a wave of such potent lust crashing over me that I have to catch myself against the counter to hold myself back from her.

Mine, mine, mine.

She's mine either way, but the thought that I'll be the only one to ever be inside her is making me desperate to stake my claim on her before someone else does.

I know there haven't been any men in her life since I've been watching her, and the thought of anyone else fucking her makes me feel homicidal.

"So, what do you do?" Her sweet voice breaks into my dark thoughts as she continues making our cups. I watch in spellbound fascination as she tucks a long strand of brown hair behind her ear. The move is so innocent, yet for some reason, it has my cock hardening inside my pants even more—so much so that it's straining against my zipper.

I try to focus on anything else. I let her make the small talk if it'll put her more at ease. Maybe it'll distract me from the rod of steel between my legs that's demanding I plow into the girl in front of me and make her mine.

I clear my throat, "I'm a co-founder of Donovan Industries."

Her eyes widen at that. She knows the name. Of course, everyone in the city does.

"Wow. That's impressive." Her eyes are big and full of admiration.

I just shrug as she hands me my cup. I take a sip of it, and creamy, sugary sweetness explodes on my tongue. I don't know why I told her I wanted a lot of cream and sugar. Well, yeah, fuck that. I do know why. I wasn't talking about the damn coffee. I was talking about *her*.

I usually take my coffee black. However, I blink and am pleasantly surprised when I actually enjoy this overly sugary drink.

I nod down at the coffee cup, "That's what's impressive, lass." And it truly is. If she can make someone like me, who is a stout black coffee drinker, like this overloaded cup of sugar, then she's definitely got some sort of skill.

She smiles a genuine smile that reaches her eyes. "Thanks! It's a new recipe I was trying out. I've just been playing with it, trying to get it just right."

"So, you enjoy making coffee?" I ask her, keeping up with the small talk.

Her blush deepens, and she tucks that strand of hair back behind her ear again self-consciously. "I know it might seem kind of silly, but I really do love my job. Well, I mean, I love parts of it. I would honestly like to own my own coffee shop one day, but there's no telling when—if ever—I'll be able to make that happen." She lets out little laugh. Fuck, I'd paid money to hear that laugh every day for the rest of my life.

"What would your coffee shop be like?" I ask her.

She studies me a moment as if she's trying to decide if I'm just humoring her. I'm not. I honestly want to know. I want to know everything about her. Her hopes and dreams. Every thought that passes through her head.

She obviously detects my sincerity because she begins animatedly laying out her ideas. I can't stop staring at the way her eyes light up when she's talking about something she's obviously excited about.

If I thought she was beautiful before, she's even more so now. She catches me staring at her again, and she apologizes, "I'm rambling. I'm sorry. I tend to do that. Just ignore me if I get on your nerves." She lets out another nervous laugh.

"You're fine, Rachel," I tell her, "and I don't think it's silly at all. I think you're really onto something there."

"I'm a businessman first and foremost," I remind

her, "and I think you've actually got a really good idea."

Her eyes widen as she asks me hopefully, "Really?"

I nod. I'm not just telling her this because she's the woman I'm desperately in love with. It's true. She has some sound business ideas. She's obviously thought this through before. This isn't some pipe dream. This is something she's serious about, and if I thought she would take it, I would offer to be her investor.

First of all, I know Rachel's too proud to accept the offer. Secondly, with that comes a huge conflict of interest. I don't want her to refuse to get into a relationship with me just because we're going into business together.

No, it's better to get to know her personally first, and then once I convince her she's mine, I'll give her that coffee shop and anything else she wants.

I look down into her warm caramel-colored eyes before I allow my gaze to rove down, taking in her little upturned nose and her puffy pink lips.

I never imagined that today would be the day I'd actually be sitting across from my angel and having a conversation.

It's already so much more than I ever imagined it could be. I don't even have to touch her. We don't even have to be speaking. I'd be perfectly content to just sit here and stare at her all day, studying every expression that flits across her face, watching every little movement she makes.

I take another sip of the coffee Rachel made me. It wouldn't have mattered if her coffee had tasted like shit. I'd still have drunk it simply because she made it for me.

I can't help but notice the rise and fall of her chest. The slight little moans of pleasure she makes when she sips her own cup. All of these innocent little things she's doing are driving me fucking crazy. I want to pull her into my lap, hold her in my arms and never let her go.

My obsession is already knocking against the back of my mind, begging to be let out.

I grit my teeth and tighten my hands around the coffee cup. When I realize what I'm doing, I force myself to relax, slackening my jaw and releasing my grip so I don't shatter her cup.

Rachel just met me. She doesn't know me like I know her.

I keep trying to remind myself of this over and over again so that I don't act on impulse and scare her.

I can't touch her again.

Not tonight.

But soon.

Because things were set into motion tonight. Things that I know I now have no power of stopping.

I'll only be able to keep myself on a leash for so long.

And god help anyone who tries to stand in my way then—even Rachel herself.

four

Rachel

GOOD LORD, the huge Irishman looks so big in my tiny little apartment. I can't help but stare at the way his huge hand seems to wrap around one of my coffee mugs, whereas I have to hold my mug with two hands, and they still won't completely wrap around the cup.

The man is a powerhouse of raw masculinity He's practically pulsing with it.

When he finishes his cup, I reach out a hand to take it over to the sink. My fingers brush his in the process. It's just the lightest brush of his skin against mine, but it's enough to send tingles running up my arm.

I see his entire body tense as his eyes snap up to mine.

My breath catches. His green eyes are burning up at me. I stand there like a moth caught in the flame.

"Rachel," he growls out my name.

"Derrick," I whisper his name back.

A shudder goes through him, and then, lightning fast, he's standing before me. I stumble back in shock, but I don't fall because his huge arms are wrapping around me, catching me once again.

Dear god, they're so big and sinewy, and is it crazy for me to admit that I feel totally safe in them?

Yeah, that's crazy, right? Because I just met this man.

But he did save your life, a little voice in my head whispers to me.

And I might not have much—okay *any*—experience with men, but even I can pick up on the way this man is looking at me.

He's looking at me like he *wants* me. You know, in that way that a man wants a woman?

And that sends my pulse racing for several reasons.

One, the man is outrageously sexy.

Two, I can't believe a man who's this good-looking is interested in little ole' me. I mean, I'm nothing special. I'm not a model. I'm short and tiny everywhere except for my hips and breasts that seem a bit too large for my petite frame. My hair isn't a beautiful golden blonde of the sun. It's just a dull brown. I'm not glamorous by any means. In fact, I'm pretty sure that my white button-up top has a coffee stain on it right now.

Yet for some reason, this insanely hot Irishman is looking at me like he wants to devour me whole.

And dear God help me but I want him to, and that's crazy too, right? Because I don't really know anything about this man.

Yet I know that I love the way his arms feel around me.

I like the way he looks at me like he's caressing me with his eyes.

I like those flecks of red that I spot in his beard, and I can't help wondering if it's as soft as it looks and if it would be scratchy on my skin.

"Say it again, lass," he prompts me as he towers over me, still holding me in his arms. My hands are pressed against the hard pecs of his chest. My head barely comes up midway to his chest, so I'm craning my neck back to look up at him.

I lick my lips nervously. "Say what?" Were we talking about something? I can't remember. I've completely taken leave of all my senses.

All I can think about is his big arms around me and the sudden pulsing I feel at the apex of my thighs.

"My name, Rachel. Say my name," his chest rumbles under my hands.

I bite my lips, turned on beyond words at the lilting way the syllables come out of his mouth. His voice is low and gruff, and it has me instinctively pressing my thighs together, trying to ease that ache that's suddenly blossomed deep within me.

I lick my lips and peek up at him again. "Derrick," I whisper his name again, loving the taste of it on my tongue.

"Fuck me," he finally groans before he grabs the nape of my neck and crashes his lips down over mine.

I'm so stunned all I can do is stand there for a moment.

But then I register the feeling of his lips against mine, and I feel his tongue seeking entry to my mouth. I don't even think. My mouth opens on its own accord, letting him in.

And sweet baby Jesus when his tongue slips inside my mouth?

It's like my body's floodgates have been activated because moisture pools between my thighs.

He tilts my head up to him, holding me how he wants me. He groans into my mouth as he begins to stroke his tongue in and out in an obvious imitation of the sexual act.

My knees go weak, and I whimper and melt against him.

His arm bands around me, holding me tightly against him so I don't fall.

Is it pathetic that I'm twenty-one years old and this is my first real kiss? I mean, yeah, I kissed boyfriends in the past, but they were just simple pecks on the lips or one-lip kisses. I've never had a man's tongue in my mouth like this. This man is essentially tongue-fucking me and sweet baby Jesus if it's not causing moisture to flood between my thighs.

"Taste so good, sweet baby," he whispers against my lips. Then, he begins kissing along my jaw. His lips are everywhere, sliding sensuously down my neck where he proceeds to lick and suck and bite.

I moan and tilt my head to the side to grant him greater access. I swear to God if he was a vampire, I'd be in trouble right now because I'm willingly offering my neck up to anything he wants to do to me. He can bite the shit out of me. I don't care.

"Rachel, Rachel, Rachel," he chants my name like it's a prayer.

He sucks hard on the side of my neck, and I'm flooded with sensation. I never realized a man's mouth on my skin could feel so good.

His hands are pressing firmly into my back, holding me flush against him. I feel his hardness on my stomach, and good lord he feels like he's just as big there as he is everywhere else.

I know the mechanics of how sex works, but I don't know how in the world he thinks he could ever get that thing inside me.

He's so big where I'm so small, but my pussy is throbbing in tandem to the pulsing of his erection. She doesn't seem to care that he's big enough to tear her apart. She wants him anyway.

"Just let me taste you, sweet baby," he whispers as he starts kissing over my collarbone.

I gasp as he yanks my shirt open, the buttons flying every which way. Thank goodness I have plenty of backup white button-up blouses. I can't even find it in me to care that he's ruined one of my shirts, though —not whenever his big hands come up to cup my breasts, his thumbs pushing the cups down and exposing my rosy nipples that instantly pebble under his hungry gaze.

"Look at these perfect little cherries," he groans reverently, his mouth descending to capture one.

His wetness envelopes my nipple, and it shoots a tingle straight down to the little nub between my legs. He's rolling his thumb over the other nipple while he swirls his tongue around the one in his mouth. And then his mouth and hand swap places, never leaving one breast unattended.

My breasts feel fuller than they've ever felt before. And as I look down and see this huge, bearded man suckling at me, it causes something within me to clench.

"Derrick," I whisper his name, half begging but not entirely sure what I'm asking for, just that I need *something*.

"I know, baby. I know," he whispers as he starts to kiss his way down my stomach.

He drops to his knees in front of me and undoes my skirt, slowly slipping it and my panties down all at one time.

My face heats whenever his big chest expands as he inhales, smelling me. He pushes on my thighs until my butt hits the edge of the table, and then he lifts me up so that I'm lying on the table spread out before him.

"Look at that pretty little thing," he marvels as he stares at me where no one has ever seen me before. "Prettiest little thing I've ever seen in my life, I swear to god, Rachel."

I vaguely register the way he keeps saying my name so familiarly. It's like he knows me. Like he *really* knows me. Maybe I should find it odd, but I don't. Somehow it feels as if we *have* known each other our whole lives. Everything about this moment feels so right.

And when his tongue snakes out of his mouth and licks me from the bottom of my gash all the way up to my clit, my head falls back, and I let out a sound I didn't even know I was capable of making.

It encourages him because he does it again and again and again. My entire body jumps whenever his tongue passes over my little bundle of nerves at the top of my mound.

He definitely notices that too because he holds my thighs firmly in place with a big hand on each one, and then he begins to pay special attention to that area, sucking and laving on it until I'm a writhing mess, mewling and whimpering and almost sobbing.

I feel pressure building deeper and deeper within

me, and I start thrusting my hips up to his face, seeking out more of his tongue.

"Let it go, sweet baby. Give me everything you got," he encourages me.

My breathing becomes hot and ragged. I can feel tendrils of my hair sticking to my skin. I feel like I'm right on the brink of something wonderful.

He sucks on my clit hard one last time. I explode, tingles racing all throughout my entire body and my limbs. I cry out, and he continues sucking and licking me, drinking up all the moisture that floods from between my legs.

"Sweetest cream I've ever tasted, baby," he growls against me. "All I'll ever need to sweeten my coffee. Goddamn, could bottle this stuff and sell it, but I'm too damn selfish. I'll be damned if I ever let anyone sample this tasty little pussy. Can't share it with anyone. Mine. All mine."

I lay there limply as I float into another dimension before slowly coming back down to earth. He's still between my legs, licking me clean, and when he raises his head, I can see my juices glistening in his beard and on his lips.

I sit up and then lean into Derrick, hiding my face in his chest.

"Derrick, that was...that was..." I stumble over my words, "I mean, I've never..."

He tilts my head up with a finger on my chin, his eyes heated as he confirms, "That was your first orgasm."

I nod shyly, blushing at my admission. I start to look down in shame, but he forces me to meet his eyes.

"I fucking *love* that I gave you your first, sweet baby. And if I have my way, I'll be the one to give you your last and every one leading up to it."

The way he's looking at me so tenderly yet so possessively has me feeling all warm and fuzzy inside, and suddenly I want to make him feel just as good as he made me feel.

I start unbuttoning his shirt. He watches me with heated eyes, dragging in a ragged breath as I pass my fingers over his bare skin. The muscles of his chest and stomach ripple as I trail my fingertips over him.

When I finally get his shirt all the way unbuttoned, he helps me slip it off his shoulders. Acting on instinct, I lean in and kiss the broad expanse of his chest.

He curses and fists his hands in my hair when I press my lips against his skin. "Fuck, baby, you're going to kill me." His breathing comes out in heavy puffs as I continue to kiss his chest, trailing my lips down over his stomach.

I reach the waistband of his pants and start to unbuckle him, but he stills my hand by placing his own over mine. I look up at him questioningly, my cheeks suddenly red. Is he turning me away? Did I misread everything? Does he not really want me?

He shakes his head down at me, his throat working.

"Rachel," he finally croaks out, "baby, are you sure you want to do this?"

Relief immediately floods me. It's not that he doesn't want me.

I bite my lip and nod up at him, suddenly never surer of anything in my entire life.

I do. I want this. I want my first time to be with this man. This man who saved my life and who I somehow inexplicably trust. I don't know how I know, but I know that he's the one who's meant to be my first. I trust him to be the one to take my virginity and make me a woman.

"Yes," I whisper, holding eye contact with him so he can see that I mean what I say.

His pupils dilate, and his nostrils flare, but he still keeps his hand on top of mine.

"There's something you should know, baby," his

words are low and serious, his brogue thicker than ever. "If we do this, there's no going back. Ye're going to be mine and only mine. Do you understand what I'm saying to ye, lass?" His eyes are smoldering down at me with fierce possessiveness, and it causes a shiver to run up my spine.

Suddenly, I want nothing more than to be his. I nod my head, agreeing to his terms.

Something within him seems to snap then. His chest heaves as he starts unbuckling his pants. Something about those big hands working that buckle has me biting my lips and clenching my thighs together again.

He curses when he notices. "Got such a horny little girl on my hands, don't I? Needs this cock."

My cheeks heat at his words, but they only cause me to pulse even more.

He quickly shucks off his pants, his thick, swollen ridge of flesh bobbing free. My eyes widen when I take in the naked length and girth of him. Not only is he long, but he's impossibly thick too. I bite my lip, starting to have second thoughts about whether he'll fit or not.

He must sense my worry because he tilts my head up to look at him and kisses me gently. "It'll fit baby, I promise," he reassures me. "I'll go slow."

"Okay," I nod, trusting him.

He lays me back on the table and then positions his tip at my entrance.

He begins to push in very slowly. My eyes widen at the sensation of just his fat tip pushing inside me. I wince at the feeling of being stretched so impossibly wide, but he bends over and begins kissing me softly, his tongue slipping leisurely in and out of my mouth.

I feel more wetness pool between my thighs in response to his kisses. His hands are petting all over my skin, stroking me, petting me.

All the while he's still slowly pressing inside me, filling me deeper and deeper until he suddenly stops.

I look up at him in surprise. That's it? Wow, that really wasn't so bad. Not as bad as I'd heard it was. Yeah, it was a bit uncomfortable, but nothing like the pain I've heard some girls have.

I relax, relieved that the worst of it is over.

He doesn't say anything at first. His jaw is clenched tightly, and he grabs hold of my hip.

"Look in my eyes, sweet baby," he finally grits out.

I instantly obey, my eyes finding his. I marvel at all the different shades of green swirling within them. He really does have such beautiful eyes.

Suddenly, he plunges deep inside me. I let out a

scream at the intense sensation of being ripped in half.

Instantly, he's all around me, his big arms framing me in on either side as he hunches over me. I'd only thought he was all the way inside before.

Now, I feel him deep within me, my tiny hole more stretched than I ever thought possible.

"Jesus," he groans out before he cups my face. "Ssh, baby. Rachel, baby," he's dropping tiny kisses on my lips as he apologizes for my pain.

"I didn't want to hurt you, baby, but I had to get in this perfect little pussy. Had to. So perfect. So perfect," he mumbles.

He moans a deep guttural sound but holds himself still inside me as he begins stroking over my hair and soothing me. Dropping little kisses all over my forehead and my cheeks before coming back to kiss my lips, softly taking my mouth in gentle one-lip kisses and then slipping his tongue inside my mouth. "So perfect," he continues to whisper words of praise in my ear. "More perfect than I ever could have imagined."

The pain finally starts to subside, and then I suddenly become very aware of his heavy weight inside me and how it's pulsing within me.

It's creating a pulse within me too, and I feel myself tighten around him involuntarily.

He groans, the muscles in his neck going taut as he feels my muscles clenching around him.

"Oh my god," he pants. "Can't sit still anymore. Gotta move baby. Pussy's gripping me so mother-fucking tight."

I nod and wrap my arms around his neck, silently giving him permission.

He pulls my leg up beside him and grips the side of my thigh as he begins to pull out and push back in, slowly at first and then with increasing tempo.

Every time he stabs back inside me he hits this spot deep within me that sends tingles shooting all throughout my core.

Before I know it, I'm thrusting up at him trying to get more of that sensation.

He stutters out a breath before groaning, his eyes half wild as he starts to shower me with praises again. "Look at you. So perfect. Taking me so perfectly. Throwing that thing back up on me. You know this is your cock. Don't you?" He punctuates his words with stab after stab. "You know that little pussy was made for this cock, don't you?"

I let out a keening sound, and he groans deep in his throat.

"That's it, baby. That's it." He continues to plunge in and out of me. "Give it to me. Just like that, honey, just like that."

I do as he says, driven by an instinct I can't control, seeking my own release as well. Something tells me it's going to be way more intense than the release he gave me with his mouth earlier.

He huffs and puffs and begins taking in big, stuttering, ragged breaths.

"Oh God. Yes, Rachel. Just like that baby. You keep riding my big dick like that I'm fixing to bust this big nut all in you. I've got so much cum in these balls just for you, baby. Been holding it all back just for you. Just for you. You want it?"

His eyes are feral now as he grabs my neck and forces me to look at him.

Something about the feeling of his big palm on my neck, knowing that he holds my life in his hands heightens my pleasure.

"Tell me you want my cum," his voice is slurred, his brogue so thick I can hardly make out what he's saying. "Tell me you want this big nut."

"I want it," I moan out, never meaning anything more, wondering what it's going to feel like to feel him flooding inside of me.

I don't have to wait much longer because with

two more pumps, I suddenly feel a gush of warm fluid rocketing up in me just as I shatter all around him.

It couldn't be more perfect. We fall apart together, him spasming inside me, me convulsing around him, our juices flooding and combining until they're leaking out of my hole and all over the table.

"Oh, fuck baby. Fuck, fuck!" he curses "Here it is, honey. Take this big nut. All for you, lass. All for you!"

His filthy words send me into another orgasm. I feel myself clench around him again, tightening and releasing around him over and over again.

He groans long and deep like his soul is being ripped from him as he buries his face in my neck, his whole body shuddering over me as he holds himself deep, spraying rope after rope of thick, sticky seed inside me.

I can feel the jets coating my womb with his essence.

Just knowing that I caused this big, powerful man to fall apart like this fills me with a sense of complete feminine satisfaction.

"Rachel, baby. My Rachel," he's whispering against my ear as he strokes my hair and kisses all over my face, holding me tenderly.

"Mine," he's rasping against me. "Addicted. I'm

never going to let you go now, honey. Pretty little girl... just sealed your fate...never get rid of me now."

I let him hold me and whisper words of possession in my ears, basking in the feeling of finally belonging to someone.

If he wants to keep me, that's okay with me.

Because for once, I don't care about being independent. For once, I want to be kept.

I want to be his.

five

Derrick

THIS IS IT.

Rachel is mine.

Mine, mine, mine.

The words are reverberating in my head to the beat of my heart.

I couldn't leave her last night. After I picked her up and carried her from the kitchen to her bedroom, we just laid on her bed entangled in each other's arms, breathing together, neither of us speaking. There aren't enough words in the English language—or any language for that matter—to capture what passed between us.

I held her until she drifted off to sleep curled up against my chest like a little kitten. I don't know how long I stared down at her. It could have been minutes. It could have been hours.

All I know is that I marveled at the feeling of finally having her willingly nestled up against me. Like she belonged there, and she does. This is right where she belongs. Right here in my arms. I'm already awake, but she's still sleeping. I'm watching the way her eyelashes flutter over her cheeks and how her little lips are slightly parted in sleep.

I run a hand through her hair, marveling at the silky texture of it once again. She's so soft and silky all over. I can't get enough of her. I can't stop touching her. When my hands skim over her shoulder and down her arm, her eyes finally flutter open. She smiles up at me sleepily, her cheeks turning a light pink when she realizes I've been watching her.

"Good morning," she murmurs in that husky little voice of hers.

"Good morning, sweet baby." I drop kisses on her eyes.

"How long have you been awake?" she peers up at me.

"Not long," my voice comes out as a low rumble.

She stretches languorously. "What time is it?"

I know that it's technically past time for me to already be on my way to the office. And I also know that she's usually up and moving by now too. But I just wanted more time with her in my arms. That's why I couldn't bring myself to wake her even when I knew I should have.

I tell her the time.

"Oh shit, I'm going to be late if I don't start moving right now," she bolts upright in the bed, forgetting her nudity at first. When she realizes it, her cheeks flush pink again, and she pulls the sheet up to cover her.

I pull it back down with a growl. I'm having none of that. "Never try to hide your body from me, Rachel. You're beautiful."

Her blush only deepens, and she smiles at me shyly as a curtain of hair falls over her shoulder to hide her face.

"Don't you have to be getting to work too?" she asks me curiously.

I shrug. "I'm co-owner, so I'm flexible. I can pretty much do what I want." I wink at her. "Being your own boss has those perks."

She giggles and grins at me. "Yeah, I guess it does, but some of us don't have those luxuries."

She lithely steps out of the bed and hurries to the bathroom, no doubt trying to get there as quickly as she can. She's still not completely comfortable walking around naked in front of me. Poor girl doesn't know that thanks to the cameras I installed in her home, I've seen her strutting around in her pretty little panties and nothing else more times than I can count.

Should I feel bad for invading her privacy like that? Probably.

Do I? No.

I frown when I hear the shower running, not liking the thought that she's going to be washing me off her skin.

Call me a Neanderthal, but I like the thought of her being covered in my cum while she's working all day. I want her marked. I want everyone to know she's mine.

I follow her into the shower, and she lets out a little jump when my arms circle her from behind.

I start kissing the side of her neck, and she moans, tilting her head to the side, exposing more of her creamy flesh to my lips.

"Derrick, I can't," she lets out a little whimpering

moan that sends fire flooding through my veins. "I'll be late for work."

Her protests are weak at best. I hear the words she's saying, but her body's pressing back into me, telling me a whole different story.

"We'll be quick, baby," I say as I slip into her from behind, too hard up for her now.

She gasps and doesn't resist me as I impale her on my hard length.

"Oh god," she moans, no doubt feeling how much bigger I feel from this position. I feel it too. My entire body is shuddering. She feels even tighter like this, her pussy gripping me like a vice.

I don't waste any time and begin plowing up into her while my hand reaches around to stroke her wet, slippery clit.

I'm only five pumps in whenever I feel that familiar churning in my balls.

"Fuck," I groan, grabbing her wet hair and pulling her head back, needing to look in her pretty brown eyes as I pop off inside her.

When I feel the first rush of release shooting up my stalk, I smash my lips down onto hers wildly, taking them in a bruising kiss.

I hold back as long as I can, rubbing her clit furiously, trying to coax her over the edge with me.

Finally, the pressure becomes too much, and I release with a deep groan as I begin to flood inside her.

I feel her fall apart on me the moment my seed bursts up into her. Her tight little muscles are squeezing and milking and sucking at me greedily, and I groan into her mouth as my hand slaps onto the shower wall to hold myself up.

My motherfucking knees go weak, and I reach over and turn off the shower head before I collapse, taking us down to the tile floor where I settle her on my lap, my cock still inside her, jerking with aftershocks.

I move my lips to her neck again, this time sucking hard with the sole intention of getting all her blood to pool to the surface to leave a visible mark on her.

I wonder if she'll be pissed at me for it later. It doesn't really matter either way. At this point, I'm lost to my madness and don't really care. She's going to wear my mark one way or the other. I *need* her to.

I want every other male who sees her to know that she's taken. Claimed. Possessed. *Mine.* I tighten my hold on her hips possessively, only loosening up when she starts to squirm in discomfort.

When she finally entangles herself from me and stands, she reaches for the washcloth to clean up, but I still her hand.

"Don't wash me off you," I order her, my voice coming out gruff.

She stills and looks at me in confusion. "But—" she starts to protest, but I stand to tower before her, placing a finger on her lips.

I lean down so that my eyes are only inches from hers as I tell her honestly, "I want to know that pussy is dripping with me all day long. I want you to feel me inside you all day and know that tonight I'm going to fill you up again. I'm going to keep you so full of my cum you'll be dripping for days, baby."

My voice comes out hoarse with my passion. Christ, I sound insane. I clench my jaw together and have to physically hold myself back from burying myself inside her again.

She stares up at me slack-jawed, no doubt shocked at my words, but I see the way her thighs clench, so I know that they turn her on just as much as they do me.

Is it twisted? Probably.

Do I give a fuck? Most certainly not.

Hell, I've even surprised myself with the filth that comes out of my mouth when I'm around her, but I can't help it. All of my filters fly off when I'm in her presence, and all I can think about is making her mine. Making her see that she's mine. Making her feel this intensity as much as I do.

This is why I held back for so long. This is why I merely watched her for so long. I knew I wouldn't be able to control myself with her.

She drops the washrag, her face flushing as she obeys me. Christ, the thought of my cum dripping down her thighs all day while she works has my cock swelling again.

She steps out of the shower and begins drying off. My eyes are riveted to her. I couldn't look away if I tried.

My chest is rising and falling rapidly with my ragged breaths. Everything I'm feeling for her is so intense. It's swirling and twining all around in my chest, making it tighter and tighter until I feel like I'm going to burst.

"Derrick, I..." she pauses and shakes her head, searching for words. My eyes drop down to the towel she's holding up at her breasts, and my nostrils flare. I'm tempted to rip it from her body and drive inside her again. Fuck her senseless until she promises that she's mine, only mine.

"This is just...I don't know..." she chews on her bottom lip, and I groan. Her eyes flick back up to me. "It's all just so crazy, isn't it? I mean, we just met last night, but I feel like I've known you much longer. If that makes any sense..." she trails off.

My heart skips a beat, and I latch onto her words like a lifeline. "It makes perfect sense, sweet baby."

I reach for her hand and kiss her knuckles, holding her eyes as I do so. "I feel it too. We're meant to be together, lass."

"But, I mean," she begins again, her little brow furrowing as she starts to overanalyze everything, "is this moving too fast?"

She looks up at me, looking for an answer.

I grab another towel and wrap it around my waist before I step out of the shower myself and take her face in my hands, looking directly into her eyes, willing her to listen to me. "Fuck no, baby. When you know something's right, it's right. And, lass, nothing has ever been righter than you and me."

I kiss her lips gently, rolling my tongue against hers. Her body melts up into me.

"You feel that?" I whisper against her lips. "Nothing on this goddamned earth is more right than that, sugar."

Her eyes soften, and she bites her lip.

I work to ease her mind even more, though, tilting her face up so that she has to look into my eyes once more. "Anything you want to know about me, you just ask. We have the rest of our lives to learn everything there is to know about each other."

She's looking up at me so trustingly, and it's like a punch to my gut.

"I already know all that I need to know, though, Rachel," I tell her earnestly. "I know that I want you and only you. Yesterday? It wasn't a coincidence, sweet baby. That was fate's way of throwing us together. And who are we to tempt fate?"

She's looking up at me with wide eyes now as she processes what I've said.

I feel a stab of guilt whenever I think of how I'm technically manipulating circumstances to my advantage. She's going to think that our meeting was some serendipitous encounter when really I've been stalking her for weeks now.

But it was still fate, right? It was fate for me to walk into that coffee shop and see her. It was fate for me to become this obsessed with her so that I follow her everywhere and saw when she was about to fall into the road and was there to save her.

So, it's technically not a lie, right? It was still all some sort of fate. If you believe in sort of thing. I don't know what I believe in, but I do know I believe one thing. That Rachel is mine.

"You really believe that?" she asks me wonderingly.

"Yes, lass." I can't resist pressing my lips against her forehead. "I really believe we're meant to be together."

Her cheeks flush again. Christ, I'll never get tired of seeing her blush.

She looks up again, and I see her eyes flick over to the clock we can see from the open door of the bathroom.

She pulls away from me and starts moving in a flurry again, throwing on her typical uniform of black slacks and a white button-up blouse. She doesn't have time to dry her hair, so she just towel dries it as much as she can and pulls it up into a damp ponytail. Christ Almighty, I want to wrap that ponytail around my fist and...

I shake my head, not allowing my thoughts to go there or neither of us will ever get to work.

Primitive male satisfaction pulses in my chest when I take in the prominently visible mark on her neck. She obviously hasn't noticed it yet, and that's fine with me. I don't want her trying to cover it up with makeup or anything else.

Good. Now everyone who sees her today will know that she's taken.

"Rachel," I loop my arms around her waist and pull her against me once we're both dressed.

She looks up at me, her caramel eyes wide and innocent. "Remember who you belong to, lass," I remind her gruffly, trying to impress upon her just how much I mean those words.

I need her to understand just how serious I am about this.

She's mine and no one else's.

I can't live without her now.

One hit. That's all it took, and now I'm even more addicted than I was when I was watching her from afar.

"Mine," I repeat before I seal the words with a possessive kiss.

six

Rachel

TO SAY that Derrick is intense would be the understatement of the year. Ever since the day he literally swept me away in his arms, it's been like a whirlwind romance right out of a fairytale.

At first, my overly analytical mind was trying to pick everything apart. It was telling me that we haven't known each other long enough for our feelings to run this deeply. And the possessive glint in Derrick's eyes every time he looks at me, the way he's *so* sure that I'm his, the way he seems to instinctively know everything about me, what I like and dislike, the way he touches me like he knows my body better than I do...it's all just so much.

But after his reassuring words about how this is fate, I decided to let all my reservations go. I've always been too cautious, and I think it's kept me from really living. Besides, who I am to give my bestie, Ella, hell about not giving the guy who's been asking her out a chance when fate threw me a hot Irishman too and I hesitated? It all just seems too good to be true.

I need to follow my own advice and just take a chance. At least Ella has a good reason to be skeptical. Her piece of shit ex cheated on her just because he was too much of a horndog to wait for her when she told him she just wasn't ready to lose her virginity yet.

My face flushes when I think of how I gave it up to Derrick on the first night. It wasn't even technically a date. It was a cup of coffee to say thanks for saving my life, so what kind of sex is that even called?

Would Derrick have waited if I'd told him no? Something tells me that, yes, he would have. I know deep in my heart that Derrick would never have forced me.

Still, the way the man attacks me with his lips, almost desperately, every time he sees me...good lord, it makes my nipples pebble and that place between my legs throb just thinking about it.

It's only been a week and Derrick is just...wow. I'm convinced a man has never been as possessive of a woman as he is of me.

He insists on leaving hickeys all over my skin, most specifically my neck where everyone can see it when I have my hair up in a ponytail. I'm surprised my face didn't permanently stay as red as a tomato from all the teasing I got from my coworkers that first morning when I showed up. He'd left a mark on my neck unbeknownst to me, and I'll never be able to live it down.

But I just embrace it now, secretly loving how crazy about me he is. So what if it was fast? So what if it doesn't really make sense?

All I know is I've never felt happier than when I'm with him.

I stopped trying to cover up all his love bites, as he calls them. He growled when he saw me trying to put makeup over them one day, so I just let it go. Everyone has seen me with one mark on my neck now, right?

And really, I kind of like knowing that it's there. That he desires me so much he wants to make sure everyone knows I'm taken.

He drives me to work every day, and he's there to pick me up every day too. Some days he works in the coffee shop all day, and every time I look up, I find his eyes on me, watching my every move.

Maybe I should find his fixation on me disturbing, but I don't.

I actually find it comforting.

Like with him always watching me, I'm safe. Cherished. Adored.

Most nights we stay at his place now. I was so awed by his view of the city that I'm surprised my jaw didn't hit the floor.

On the nights when I insist on going home, he always joins me. It's like he never wants to be separated from me now.

And I'm honestly okay with that because I don't want to be away from him either.

I finish filling my last order for the day before I remove my apron and get ready to leave. Derrick will be here any minute, so I sit at an empty table and rest my aching feet while I wait for him. My toes curl just thinking about the magnificent way Derrick massages my feet for me. He does it every day I work. I've never asked him to, but it's like he can sense my discomfort and seeks to ease it however he can.

That's just...so Derrick. He's always staying one step ahead of me, anticipating my needs—even those that I don't know I have—and always doing his best to fulfill them.

I swear he's spoiling me.

I look up with a smile when a shadow passes over me, assuming it's Derrick.

It's not. My smile fades a bit, but I try to hide my disappointment. I don't want to look like a bitch and put off customers.

I recognize the guy as the last customer I made a coffee for. He's wearing an expensive business suit and smiling down at me. I suppose his brown eyes and blonde hair are attractive enough, but he's not Derrick, so his charming smile and good looks do nothing for me.

He introduces himself, but I'm so distracted thinking about Derrick that I don't catch his name. Oh well, hopefully I won't have to remember it or say it.

"...and I was wondering if you'd like to have dinner with me sometime?" I tune back in just in time to hear him ask me out.

Oh, wow. This is awkward. I open my mouth to let the guy down as gently as possible.

But I never get the chance to because a completely unamused voice growls threateningly from right behind me, "Fuck off. She's taken."

I suddenly feel Derrick's hands land on my shoulders possessively. He pulls my hair back to fall over my shoulder, effectively revealing his mark on my neck.

I see Mr. what's-his-name's eyes flick down to my neck. His lips press into a thin line, and he takes a step back, murmuring an apology.

Derrick doesn't say a word. He just keeps glaring at the guy like a wolf with his back raised, every hair standing on end.

He's marking his territory. Defending his mate.

It's archaic, and maybe the feminist in me should balk at being claimed in such a primitive fashion, but the side of me that's a slut for everything Derrick is swooning.

I clench my thighs together under the table, suddenly throbbing.

"You ready, lass?" Derrick asks me. The fire of anger is still blaring in his eyes as he looks down at me.

I just nod, unable to speak.

He gently pulls me up from the chair and leads me outside to where his driver is waiting.

Yes, Derrick is *that* rich that he has his own personal driver. Sometimes he likes driving, though, and drives himself, but most of the time, he has someone else drive us so he can sit in the back with me.

No sooner do we get in the car does Derrick press the button to raise the glass separating the driver from us, his eyes never leaving mine.

As soon as we're obscured from the driver's view, he pounces on me, smashing his lips onto mine in a bruising kiss, his hands fisting in my hair.

"Do you know what it does to me to see another man trying to steal what's mine?" he rasps against my lips, his body vibrating.

I can feel his hands shaking against my scalp, and I stroke my palms on either side of his face, stroking down his cheek all the way over his soft beard like I'm soothing a rabid animal. "No one can steal me away. I'm yours, Derrick," I press my lips against him again, seeking to reassure him.

He groans into my mouth and deepens the kiss. "I can't ever lose you, Rachel," he whispers to me. "I'd go insane without you."

"You're not going to lose me," I tell him softly, wondering where all this is coming from. Surely, it's not all brought on by one guy asking me out? And surely he knows I was going to tell him no?

His green eyes find mine, looking worried and pained and unsure. "I just can't bear the thought of losing you, lass. Promise me. Promise me you'll never leave me."

His eyes are half-wild, and though I don't really understand his reaction to one little incident, I do everything in my power to put his fears at ease. "I promise, Derrick. I'll never leave you. I love you."

His pupils dilate, and his nostrils flare when I drop the three words that have been dancing around in my head for days. I blush, wondering if it was too soon to say them.

"Say it again, lass," his brogue is so thick his voice almost sounds slurred like he's drunk.

"I love you," I whisper again, my heart soaring when the most beautiful smile I've ever seen breaks across his face.

"I love ye too, lass. My god, how I love ye." He pulls me onto his lap to straddle him and then kisses me deeply, his tongue dancing with mine.

I melt into him and feel his hardness prodding at me where I'm sitting on him.

"Can't wait," he grits out. "Gotta have you now, sweet baby."

The next thing I know he's ripping my pants down and unzipping his pants at the same time. He doesn't even bother with my panties. He just pulls them to the side before thrusting up into me to the hilt.

I let out a loud moan as he fills me so completely, my head falling back, exposing my neck to him like an offering.

And he takes it, latching onto my neck and sucking hard as he begins to drive up into me while pulling me down on him, going deeper than he's ever gone before.

I'm so wet our bodies are making squelching noises where they smash together. The driver can probably hear everything, but we're both beyond caring.

In no time, I feel Derrick swelling inside me. I crash before he does, my release ripping through me like a tidal wave.

"Fuck, yes, lass," he rasps against my neck before biting down with a guttural groan as his heat begins to flood me.

"I love ye, Rachel. I love ye. I love ye," he tells me over and over again as he strokes my hair, my back, my face, my entire body.

I cling to him, soaking up his love, basking in his adoration. I've never felt closer to another person in my entire life.

Derrick is my soulmate. I'm convinced of it. He was right. We're fated to be together. He was placed at the perfect place at the perfect time to save me.

He saved more than just my life that day. He saved me from missing out on the greatest love I've ever known.

Nothing can ever tear us apart.

I'm lying in Derrick's bed, which is admittedly way more luxurious and comfortable than mine. Of course, everything in his penthouse is way more luxurious than the thrift store finds in mine. But I don't care about any of that. All I care about is the man himself. Derrick could be dirt poor, and I still know that I would want him with every fiber of my being. That's no lie.

I stretch, savoring the feeling of his two thousand count Egyptian cotton sheets. Well, I don't know if they're really two thousand count, but I guarantee they're probably the highest count you can get on freaking sheets.

Because one thing I've learned about Derek in the short time that I've known him is that he does nothing halfway. He goes all out on everything. His appearance, his clothes, his things, me—most especially me. My mind drifts lazily back to the three orgasms he just gave me since we've been here. We were barely in the door before he was hoisting me in his arms again, his lips seeking mine. The man is insatiable.

And I love it.

I love *him*.

I feel a smile tugging at my lips as I fling my arms wide. My hand hits something sitting on his night-stand. I hear a thump as whatever it was falls to the floor.

Oops.

I peek over the side of the bed, instantly relieved to see that I haven't made a mess by knocking over a drink or something. It's just his phone.

I bend out of the bed with my feet sticking up in the air to grab the phone and put it back on his nightstand.

I don't intend to snoop on his phone. That's just not me. I'm not that kind of woman.

However, when my finger swipes across the screen as I pick the device up, I can't help glancing down.

And what I see causes me to go completely still.

I'm frozen in place, staring down at his phone as my mind slowly registers just exactly what I'm looking at.

Horror starts to creep over me, and pinpricks run up and down my spine. There are about six tiny little squares on the screen, and in each square there is a different view.

Of my apartment.

One is my bedroom. One is my kitchen. One is my living room. One is my bathroom One is my hallway. One is right outside my door.

Cameras. He has cameras up in my apartment.

I can't stop staring down at the feeds even though there's nothing to see since there's no movement going on in my empty apartment.

My mind casts around desperately for answers. Why would he have cameras up? We're never apart. Ever since that first day we met, he's slept with me at my place or I've slept with him at his place. What need would he have to have cameras up?

And then it suddenly hits me. Chills run down my spine as I continue to stare down at the phone in my hand.

These cameras can't be new. These cameras were up way before we met.

Derrick has been watching me before I ever knew him.

That's the only explanation.

I couldn't be more shocked if someone dumped a bucket of ice on my head right now.

I feel my entire body starting to shake.

I feel numb.

Everything I thought I knew about our relationship is a lie.

I thought nothing could tear us apart

But apparently, I was wrong.

Something can.

Derrick himself.

seven

Derrick

I COME out of the bathroom, my heart light. I'm ready to take my Rachel in my arms again.

I'm going to hold her all night long. She said she loved me. My chest swells at the thought.

She loves me. How did I ever get this lucky?

I'm humming an old Irish ballad as I make my way back into the bedroom, ready to slip beneath the sheets and feel my woman pressed up against me.

I instantly know something is wrong when I walk in and see Rachel staring down at my phone in her hand, her face ashen and drained of all color.

The hairs on the back of my neck rise as my stomach drops with dread.

She turns devastated eyes up to me and whispers, "You bastard."

Somehow that whisper is way louder than if she had screamed at me. One look into her eyes and I already know what she's found.

I stand there perfectly still as my sins finally find me out.

"How long?" she asks me, her voice coming out louder and shriller with each syllable she utters. "How long have you been watching me?"

My chest clenches tight, and I rub at it to try to ease the ache. *Fuck! Not now! Not now!* my mind is screaming at me. Not when Rachel finally admitted she loves me.

"It's not what you think, lass," my excuse sounds lame even to my own ears. And it's a lie. It's exactly what she thinks. It's exactly what it looks like. I was watching her without her knowledge. I've been stalking her.

I see the puzzle pieces snapping together inside her brain. "That day on the street," she speaks very slowly as she pieces it all together. "It wasn't fate," she turns grief-stricken eyes up at me. "You didn't just happen to be there at the right place at the right time.

You were there because you've been watching me. You've been stalking me," she whispers that last bit with all the horror my actions deserve.

I take a cautious step toward her, but she crawls backwards across the bed to put distance between us. My heart wrenches within me to see her retreating from me, cowering like she's afraid I'm going to hurt her.

"Don't come any closer," she whispers as she stands from the bed and begins hurriedly dressing, keeping her circumspect eyes on me the whole time like I'm a predator that's going to pounce on her as soon as she turns her back.

My heart breaks at the wary look in her eyes.

"Rachel, love," I plead. "Let me explain."

"There's nothing to explain," she shakes her head, her pretty brown hair mussed by the sex we've just had. She looks so beautiful I ache just looking at her.

I hate to see her looking so broken.

Because of me.

"I've seen enough." She gestures down at the phone. "It's all right there in black and white. Literally." Her eyes flick down at the camera feeds on my phone screen, which are indeed in black and white.

I slip my own shorts on and then begin taking cautious steps over to her, desperate to have her listen to me, to make her understand I don't mean her any harm. I never have.

I can't bear to see her looking at me this way. Like I've betrayed her. Like I'm some sort of freak. A monster to be feared.

"No!" she finally screams when I reach out a hand to touch her. She holds up a hand and steps back from me. "Just leave me alone, Derek."

She's inching her way toward the door, and panic flares in my chest.

"You said you'd never leave me, Rachel," my voice comes out on a croak. My chest is so tight I'm surprised I don't have a heart attack. "You promised."

She lets out an incredulous laugh, and I suppose it is a ridiculous card for me to play, trying to hold her to her promise after what I've done.

"Our whole relationship is based on a lie," her voice breaks, her lips trembling.

"Rachel," I fall to my knees shamelessly. I have no pride or shame anymore. I'll beg her. "You are my entire world." I hold her eyes, willing her to see the truth in them. "I'll make it up to you. I'll do anything lass."

She looks down at me, her eyes shimmering with tears. She shakes her head sadly. "You've already done enough."

And then she turns and nearly sprints out the door.

I physically feel the ache increasing the more distance she puts between us. My entire body is shaking as I fight the urge to run after her.

Part of me is telling myself to do it. To grab her and forcibly hold her and keep her here. She'll come around eventually.

But there's another part of me that says she'll hate me. She'll never forgive me. My heart twists inside me. I can't have Rachel hate me. Even if it means I have to lose her. I can't truly trap her and make her miserable.

I can't remember the last time I cried, but sobs wrack my body now.

How the fuck am I supposed to let her go? She's in my blood, embedded deep within my soul. Pain unlike anything I've ever known rips through me. My chest is heaving. I feel like I can't breathe.

I curl my hand into a fist and rear back before I blindly pound it into the wall. I barely register the pain shooting up my arm as my knuckles split.

I'm seething with rage and frustration, shaking with so many volatile emotions. I can't keep all this pent up inside. I'll go fucking insane.

I let out a maniacal laugh at that thought. Hell, I'm going to go insane without her anyway.

I need to hit something, something solid.

I tear myself up off the floor and stumble blindly to my exercise room where I find just what I need. I start wailing on the punching bag there. I don't even take the time to put on gloves. I just hit it over and over and over again with my bare fist, roaring as I do so.

Still, I'm not satisfied. I want to feel bone crushing beneath my hands. I want to feel the give of skin under my knuckles as I beat the living shit out of somebody.

I want to feel the pain as my opponent's hit connects with my jaw.

I haven't felt this kind of rage and bloodlust since my boxing days back in Ireland. I swore to myself I would never let myself lose control like that again.

But that was back when I was halfway sane. Back when I still had hope for living.

When Rachel walked out of that door, she took away my last shred of sanity and humanity.

I have no reason for living anymore.

I am nothing now.

Nothing but a pathetic beast.

Might as well act like one.

eight

Rachel

I'M CRYING into Ella's pillow, my shoulders heaving with deep, heart-wrenching sobs. I feel like someone has stabbed me straight through the heart.

I confessed that I loved Derrick, and to find out that he betrayed me like this is like no pain I've ever experienced before.

I make a mental note that I'm going to have to buy Ella some new sheets after blubbering all over hers like the pathetic mess that I am.

I certainly couldn't go back to my own apartment, not knowing that Derrick had cameras up everywhere and that he could watch me crying my heart out over him. I don't want him to see the blubbering mess that he's reduced me to.

It's been three days. Three agonizing days since I walked out of Derrick's place. This is the longest I've gone without feeling his arms around me since the day he saved my life.

He comes into the coffee shop every day. But as soon as I see him or feel his eyes on me, I retreat into the back, hiding like a coward. I just can't face him. Not whenever I'm still so shaken up over everything. Not when I still don't know how to feel.

He blew up my phone that first night with calls and texts, but I ignored him. I just can't face him yet, not even over the phone.

I eventually just turned my phone off and haven't turned it on since.

Ella has pretty much completely moved in with Thomas, so she was more than willing to let me stay at her place.

Of course, she's completely sympathetic to my plight and offered to come over and stay with me like a good bestie, but I'm not going to pull her from her happy ever after just because mine came crashing down around me

Besides, I honestly just need to be alone anyway. I want to wallow in my own self-pity and stupidity.

How could he have kept something like this from me? All that talk about us being fated...

He said all of that knowing damn well that he'd been watching me before we officially met.

What if he had told you? a little voice inside my head says. *You would have gone running the other way and never would have given him a chance*, it answers for me.

No, I try to tell myself, *I would have respected his honesty.*

Even I don't believe my argument. I probably would have been freaked out. Hell, I'm in love with the man and I'm completely freaked out now.

But does that change how I feel about him? Does that change how he feels about me?

Derrick really does love me.

Does he love you? another voice asks me, or *is he just obsessed with you?*

Is there a difference?

If he loves you, would he have lied to you and betrayed you like this?

He didn't exactly lie to me. He just never told me. It's a technicality sure, but if I'm the judge, aren't I the one who determines whether to cut him some slack or not? Do I want to?

I just want things to go back to the way they were, but can they ever? Can I ever get past this?

My head is swimming with all the thoughts swirling around in it like a whirlpool. I can't keep up with them.

I'm so confused I don't know what to think or feel.

I don't know how to deal with all of this.

I quiet when I hear a knock at the door.

My heart begins to race with uncertainty. I know it can't be Ella because if it was her, she would just walk in with her key. And surely it's not Derrick because I didn't tell him where I was going. Of course, I guess he has enough resources to find out where I am if he really wants to. Who knows how long he was stalking me or what all he knows about me?

A masculine voice comes through the door. "It's me." I relax only marginally whenever I hear Ella's boyfriend. He's Derrick's business partner and best friend. What if it's a ploy to get me to open the door and then Derrick will be standing there?

"You don't have to worry. I'm alone, lass," he reassures me as if he can read my thoughts.

I can't very well turn Ella's boyfriend away. Not

whenever she was nice enough to let me stay in her place.

I begrudgingly walk over and open the door. I know I must look like shit with my red-rimmed puffy eyes, tear-stained cheeks, and messy hair, but I can't find it within me to care.

Thankfully, Thomas doesn't make small talk or waste any time in getting right to what he came for. "Look, Rachel, I don't know you that well, and I'm not trying to get involved in you and Derrick's relationship and sway you one way or the other. I won't take much of your time."

He stops to rub the back of his neck, looking uncomfortable before he plows on, "I just thought you needed to know that Derrick's not doing good at all. He won't come into work. He won't accept anyone's calls. He won't see anyone. He won't listen to anyone. It's like he's gone completely off the deep end."

I look down at my feet uncomfortably. I know why he's telling me this. He's implying it's my fault that Derrick is doing this. But what about what Derrick did to me?

Thomas huffs out a long breath before confessing, "I've only ever seen him like this once before. And that was back in Ireland when his gran died. He took up boxing to help channel his rage and frustration into something, but he got out of hand."

I peek a curious look up at Thomas. I knew that Derrick had a punching bag in his workout room, but I didn't know he ever actually boxed other people.

Thomas' eyes take on a haunted look. "When Derrick fights, lass, something happens to him. He completely loses his head. He gets out of control. It took five men to pull him off his last opponent and keep him from killing him."

Thomas shakes his head and looks off into the distance as the memories assault him. "We came over here for a fresh start him and I, and Derrick has done a good job of keeping his temper reined in. He's been a lot calmer, a lot more low key, since we've been here in the States."

He levels a look down at me, "But a tiger doesn't change its stripes. He's still got that beast inside him. And I heard through the grapevine that he's slated to fight in one of the underground rings tonight."

My eyes widen as I look up at Thomas with fear. "Now, I can only imagine where his head's at, lass. He's been drinking like crazy. I can't talk any sense into him. He hasn't fought in years, and I know Derrick's a big guy, and I know what a formidable opponent he is. But I also know what he thinks he lost, and I'm afraid he could turn self-destructive too. They don't fight fair in the underground. They fight dirty. No holds barred. If Derrick doesn't go murder the other guy, he could very well be murdered himself, lass."

I gasp at the thought of Derrick dying or of him killing anyone else in his rage.

Thomas looks down at me gravely. "I think you're the only one who has the power to contain his beast, but you also have the power to unleash it, and you've definitely unleashed it, lass."

I chew on my lip nervously, worry suddenly consuming me.

"Derrick might even throw the fight just to punish himself because he thinks he deserves it for what he did to you," Thomas adds softly.

Alarm shoots through me then. My eyes shoot up to Thomas' concerned eyes of a best friend.

I could never live with myself if something happened to Derrick because of me.

The only thought in my head right now is for Derrick's safety. I can't bear the thought of him getting hurt, especially over me and on purpose.

"Take me to him," I tell Thomas.

✳ ✳ ✳

We pull up to Derek's building just as he's coming out the door. My heart skips a beat at the sight of him. He's unshaven, and his hair is unkempt. He's not wearing his typical business suit. Instead, he has on a pair of joggers and a white t-shirt. The t-shirt clings to this broad chest and shows off every ridge of muscle in his arms.

Thomas stops the car, and I jump out of the passenger seat and go running up to Derrick.

His eyes widen, and then he starts blinking furiously like he thinks I'm a hallucination.

He shakes his head as if to clear his vision. He clenches his fists together at his sides, and I see the muscles in his forearms bulging.

"Rachel?" he asks disbelievingly.

"Derrick, don't do this," I breathe, my voice barely more than a whisper. It's been three days since I've since him, and the sight of his huge body is assaulting my senses all over again.

My heart aches. I've missed him.

He shakes his head before he takes in a shaky breath and dips his head, "I hurt you, lass, and I deserve everything I've got coming to me. I'm a fucking asshole. There's no point in me living without you."

He looks so downtrodden and broken that I feel

my heart crack within my breast. Panic flares up in my chest when his words register. So Thomas' suspicions were right. Derrick's basically going to sacrifice himself to punish himself.

"Derrick, it's okay," I tell him gently, tears fogging my vision. "I forgive you."

His eyes soften, but he shakes his head at me sadly. "It doesn't matter, lass. I can't stop it. This obsession I have with you. You don't understand."

His eyes take on a half-crazed look as he stares down at me. "One look is all it took, and you became my whole fucking world. The last thing I ever wanted to do was hurt you. That's why I watched you for so long. That's why I held back from approaching you. I was afraid of just this. Of me overwhelming you and hurting you."

He spears his thick fingers into his hair. "My obsession isn't going away, Rachel. It's not going to get any better. It just keeps getting worse. The more I have you, the more I want you. If I could permanently sew you to my skin, I would."

I swallow at the intensity of both his gaze and his words. He's not exaggerating. He means every word he says.

His eyes flash with pain. "But to have you run from me...to have you look at me the way you did that night...it rips my fucking heart out. I can't bear to let you go, Rachel, but I'll try my damnedest if that's what you want. If that's what you need."

His voice comes out in broken pants as if it's taking everything within him to say them. He hates them, but he means them. As much as it's obviously hurting him, he would do this for me.

And just like that, I feel all of the confusion and uncertainty around my heart melting away. I suddenly realize that I don't care. I don't care if it was right what he did. I don't care if us meeting was some beautiful, serendipitous tale of fate.

I don't care about any of that. All I care about is the man standing in front of me. So heartbroken, yet still willing to do anything for me. Willing to put me first. Willing to sacrifice himself for what he thinks I want.

If that's not true love, I don't know what it is.

I fling myself into his arms, suddenly overcome with emotion. He groans and catches me against him tightly. "That's not what I want," I tell him, tears streaming down my cheeks. "I just want you. Just you, Derrick. I love you."

He pulls back and looks down at me, his eyes still pained and skeptical. "Are you sure, lass?" he asks uncertainly like I'm going to change my mind. He licks his lips before growling, "I'm insane for you. I'm willing to let you go now, but if I get you back inside me, I don't think I'll be able to summon up the strength again, so make your choice wisely."

His green eyes are blazing down at me with more intensity than I've ever seen in them, and that's saying something.

My decision made, I press my lips to his, unwilling to hear any more of his talk of letting me go. I want my obsessive, possessive over-the-top Irishman back.

And apparently all it took to get him back was the feeling of my lips pressed against his because his arms suddenly tighten around me, and he takes complete control of the kiss. "Rachel, Rachel, my life, my world," he breathes in between kisses that take my breath away.

His hands come up to cup my face as he turns my head up to look into my eyes. "Are you mine? Are you really mine?" His eyes are so hopeful and full of yearning.

He goes on desperately, "You'll never run from me again. Swear it to me, honey. You're willing to accept all of my craziness."

"I want you," I tell him, looking directly into his smoldering green eyes, watching the way the fire within them burns brighter at my words.

His big shoulders shake with emotion, and his arms band around me even tighter. "I'll never hurt you again, Rachel. I swear it. I swear on my life."

"I believe you," I tell him, happiness bursting inside me. "Now let's seal our promises with a kiss."

My beautiful, bearded Irishman's lips tip up into a smile. "I can do that, lass."

His lips touch mine, and we bury the past where it belongs, sealing our future with the press of our lips together.

It doesn't matter how we met.

All that matters is that we're together now.

We'll make our own fate.

epilogue

Three Years Later

Derrick

I SMILE to myself when I hear the sound of my wife humming floating over from behind the counter. She can't carry a tune in a bucket, my Rachel, but the sound of her carefree voice humming out a melody is the most beautiful sound I've ever heard.

It means she's content, and my chest swells with pride at knowing that my wife is happy.

She's already locked up for the night and drawn the shades, turning the sign to her coffee shop to closed.

That's right. I made damn sure Rachel got to

follow her dream of owning her own coffee shop. The Lucky Cup is booming. It's the hottest coffee shop in town with nothing but rave reviews.

And it's all due to Rachel, my wonderful wife.

The whir of the coffee grinder roars to life as she grinds up beans. She loves to experiment on new brews after hours. Her love for coffee has never waned, and she's gained quite a following on social media for her coffee-inspired memes.

It was hell when she was pregnant and couldn't drink the caffeinated java she loves so much, but just like I knew she would be, Rachel is a fantastic mother. She's always put our children first—even when they were in the womb. She only ate and drank stuff that was healthy for the babies.

I think of our rambunctious two-and-a-half-year-old boy, Will, and our precious one-year-old girl, Susie.

They're with the nanny right now. Rachel spends most of her days with them, leaving the running of her shop to her managers and employees, but at night, she likes to check in on the operations and play with new recipes.

My cock stiffens in my slacks as I come up behind her and her vanilla bean scent wafts up to me.

As much as I love our little family, I'm glad to have my wife all to myself right now.

My arms circle her from behind as I lean down to kiss the side of her neck.

She tilts her head to the side and smiles, not even startled by my presence. She could probably sense me there much like I can sense her when she's in the vicinity.

It still amazes me how strong our bond has gotten. After that first rough patch when she found out about how I stalked her before meeting her, we seemed to grow even closer. She embraced my insanity and obsession, loving even those darkest parts of me.

She pours us each a cup of her latest brew and then turns in my arms. "Cream and sugar?" she asks me with a mischievous grin. She already knows my answer.

My lips tip up wickedly. "Both."

She starts to turn to pour some cream and sugar in my cup, but I have something else in mind tonight.

I lift her effortlessly and sit her on the counter in front of me. I taste her lips, getting my dose of sugar.

My hands slide along her bare thighs, lifting her little yellow dress up. She whimpers when I brush my fingers over her soaking wet panties.

"I've had my sugar," I murmur against her skin as I

drop to my knees before her spread thighs, my mouth already salivating. "Now time for my cream."

I reach for the coffee cup and take a sip, holding the warm liquid in my mouth for a moment before I swallow it and quickly descend on her pussy, my hot tongue sucking and licking at the swollen nub that brings her so much pleasure.

She jerks under my palms that are holding her thighs open, her head falling back as she lets out a deep moan.

"Derrick," she moans my name as she forks her fingers into my hair.

I continue to lick and suck at her until she's writhing under me.

"Give me that sweet cream, baby," I encourage her before taking another sip of coffee, warming my mouth up. When I put my hot tongue on her again, she makes a keening sound, her fingers gripping my hair tightly as she starts to ride my face.

I stiffen my tongue, eager to give her what she needs.

I finally hold her still and suck her little pearl harder.

She falls over the edge, screaming my name as her sweet cream bathes my face.

I lick it all up, savoring the taste of her, my dick about to bust through my pants.

She lays there lifelessly for a moment as I lick her gently through all her aftershocks.

Finally, she sits up and pushes my head away. I pull her to her feet as I release myself from my fly, desperate to be inside her.

Before I can hoist her up into my arms, she drops to her knees before me.

Mirroring my own actions, she takes a sip of coffee and then engulfs me in her hot mouth.

Jesus Christ. I nearly jump out of my damn skin.

She takes me all the way back in her hot throat, sucking and swirling her tongue around my tip.

I'm leaking precum into her mouth, and she's drinking it all up, sucking it from me like she's sucking a smoothie through a straw.

Fuuuck...

"Can't take anymore, lass. Need you *now*." I yank her to her feet and spin her around so that her back is to me. She grips onto the counter just as I slam inside her hard.

We moan in unison, hers high-pitched, mine low.

I begin pumping into her, chest heaving. I'm driving into her so hard her feet are leaving the floor.

My balls are heavy with seed, and the thought of

dumping it all inside her until it's squelching out around us has me half-crazed with lust.

I grab her hair with both hands and pound into her like a madman, my staff swelling with my impending orgasm.

"Oh fuck, Rachel. Fuck! Gripping me so tight, baby. Gonna dump so much cum in you, sweet baby."

"Derrick!" she screams as my words push her over the edge. She begins pulsing all around me, and that does me in.

"Mine!" I choke out as I start to jerk inside her. My nut pops off so hard I almost fall over. I continue pushing up inside her as I flood her with more seed than I thought my balls were capable of holding. If I don't get her pregnant with our third child tonight, it'll be a miracle.

I pull her hair to the side and kiss the back of her neck as we both fight to catch our breath.

"Best coffee I've ever had, lass," I finally breathe into her ear.

She lets out a pretty little giggle before she agrees with me. "I think we've just invented a new thing. Coffee sex."

I let out my own amused chuckle before I growl, "You won't be offering it on your menu, though. That brew is for your husband only."

She turns in my arms and presses her sweet lips to mine, always more than willing to assuage my jealous beast when he rears his head.

"My husband only," she agrees.

THE END

Connect with Emma!

Visit Emma's website to get a FREE book you can't get anywhere else: www.authoremmabray.com.